George
and the
ragonfly

Ge'

Please
You ca
Or by

For Dad, and the camper. Love you, Sue x

First published 2009
Evans Brothers Limited
2A Portman Mansions
Chiltern Street
London W1U 6NR

Text copyright © Andy Blackford 2009
© in the illustrations Sue Mason 2009

British Library Cataloguing in Publication Data

Blackford, Andy.
    George and the dragonfly. - (Spirals)
    1. Children's stories.
    I. Title II. Series
    823.9'2-dc22

ISBN: 978 0 237 53878 1(hb)
ISBN: 978 0 237 53884 2 (pb)

Printed in China

Editor: Louise John
Design: Robert Walster
Production: Jenny Mulvanny

George and the Dragonfly

Andy Blackford
and Sue Mason

Evans

George watched a film about
lizards and snakes, and creatures
that slither in rivers and lakes.

He said to his mother, "Do you suppose, for my birthday or Christmas, I could have one of those?"

His mum shook her head.

"Most certainly not! You wanted a hamster and that's what you've got. It's me who looks after him, gives him his tea...

If you had a python, it's not hard
to see who'd have to feed him –
Daddy and me!"

"If I can't have a snake," said George to his hamster, "or a lizard or something, there's only one answer. I'll go to the jungle and live in the trees with a boa constrictor and six chimpanzees!"

So George packed a bag with some socks and some pants, and left for the Land of Man-Eating Ants.

But George had no sooner set foot in the garden, than a gorgeous green dragonfly said, "Beg your pardon! Before you go off and live in a tree, there's a couple of friends that I'd like you to see."

George followed the fly to where he was shown. Then, on its instructions, he lifted a stone.

There coiled a millipede, all shiny and black, and a bright orange beetle with stripes on its back.

George was amazed. They were brilliant and pretty – not what you'd expect in the midst of a city.

The dragonfly hovered and darted
beyond, and waited for George by
the side of a pond.

There were tadpoles and toads and a fat
friendly frog, and a great-crested newt
that lived under a log.

The dragonfly flew to a web on a shrub, where a red and green spider sat right at the hub.

Six of its legs were knitting a sweater,
while the two at the back were
writing a letter.

On a twig on a bush, the fly
landed next.

"I say! Do you mind?" said the twig,
clearly vexed.

"I'm an insect, you know – I just look
like a stick!"
George was impressed.
"That's a brilliant trick!"

"Morning, young George!"
called a big bumble bee.
"Who needs a snake when
there's all this to see?"

But the dragonfly showed him one final surprise – a beautiful grass snake with beady black eyes.

"Thank you!" said George to
his dragonfly guide. "That was
totally great." And then he sighed.

"I think I'll go home and not live in that tree. Why go to the jungle when there's all this to see?"

Why not try reading another **Spirals** book?

Megan's Tick Tock Rocket by Andrew Fusek Peters, Polly Peters
HB: 978 0237 53348 0 PB: 978 0237 53342 7

Growl! by Vivian French
HB: 978 0237 53351 0 PB: 978 0237 53345 8

John and the River Monster by Paul Harrison
HB: 978 0237 53350 2 PB: 978 0237 53344 1

Froggy Went a Hopping by Alan Durant
HB: 978 0237 53352 9 PB: 978 0237 53346 5

Amy's Slippers by Mary Chapman
HB: 978 0237 53353 3 PB: 978 0237 53347 2

The Flamingo Who Forgot by Alan Durant
HB: 978 0237 53349 6 PB: 978 0237 53343 4

Glub! by Penny Little
HB: 978 0237 53462 2 PB: 978 0237 53461 5

The Grumpy Queen by Valerie Wilding
HB: 978 0237 53460 8 PB: 978 0237 53459 2

Happy by Mara Bergman
HB: 978 0237 53532 2 PB: 978 0237 53536 0

Sink or Swim by Dereen Taylor
HB: 978 0237 53531 5 PB: 978 0237 53535 3

Sophie's Timepiece by Mary Chapman
HB: 978 0237 53530 8 PB: 978 0237 53534 6

The Perfect Prince by Paul Harrison
HB: 978 0237 53533 9 PB: 978 0237 53537 7

Tuva by Mick Gowar
HB: 978 0237 53879 8 PB: 978 0237 53885 9

Wait a Minute, Ruby! by Mary Chapman
HB: 978 0237 53882 8 PB: 978 0237 53888 0

George and the Dragonfly by Andy Blackford
HB: 978 0237 53878 1 PB: 978 0237 53884 2

Monster in the Garden by Anne Rooney
HB: 978 0237 53883 5 PB: 978 0237 53889 7

Just Custard by Joe Hackett
HB: 978 0237 53881 1 PB: 978 0237 53887 3

The King of Kites by Judith Heneghan
HB: 978 0237 53880 4 PB: 978 0237 53886 6